LJ

E
Mil

Miller, Margaret

Where does it go?

BTSB Bound to Stay Bound Books, Inc.

Margaret Miller

Where Does It Go?

Greenwillow Books, New York

My special thanks to all the children in this book who eagerly joined in the fun:
Adam Bass, Laurel Donalson, Amanda Hambrecht, Kenya Harris, Justin Kruger,
Jaclyn Miller, Gustavo Ruiz, Matthew Shifrin, and Randy Shorter.

The full-color photographs were reproduced from 35-mm Kodachrome 25 slides.
The text type is Avant Garde Gothic Medium and Demi Bold.

Library of Congress Cataloging-in-Publication Data
Miller, Margaret (date)
Where Does It Go? / by Margaret Miller.
p.   cm.
Summary: Suggests both right and wrong answers for where children
should put their socks, doll, crayons, and other possessions.
ISBN 0-688-10928-4 (trade). ISBN 0-688-10929-2 (lib.)
[1. Clothing and dress—Fiction.   2. Toys—Fiction.]   I. Title.
PZ7.M628Wh   1992   [E]—dc20   91-30160   CIP   AC

For Susan, my trusted guide,
with affection and gratitude

Where does Tavo put his socks?

Among the flowers?

On
his
nose?

On the dog's paw?

In the wading pool?

On his feet!

Where does Jaclyn put her bicycle?

In the basketball hoop?

Under the rocking horse?

On the roof?

In the clothes dryer?

In the garage!

Where does Randy put his ice cream?

In a sandwich?

On the toy truck?

On the sandal?

On the sand shovel?

In the bowl!

Where does Amanda put her book?

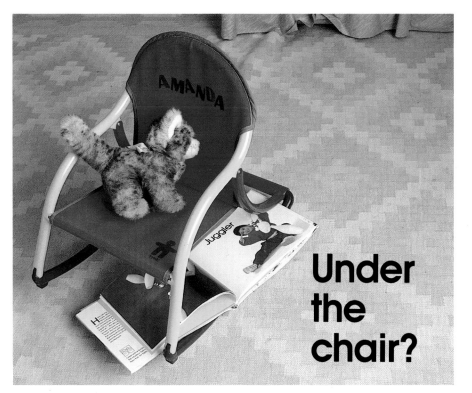

Under
the
chair?

Under the parrot?

On her baby brother?

In the mailbox?

On the shelf!

Where does Adam put his doll?

Between the peanut butter and jelly?

Behind the dog's dish?

On the piano?

In the laundry basket?

In the doll cradle!

Where does Kenya put her crayons?

In the wallet?

In her hair?

In the cat's dish?

Among the silverware?

In the box!

Where
does
Justin
put
his
toothbrush?

Through the apple?

On the teddy bear?

Among the colored pencils?

In the spaghetti?

In his mouth!

Where does Laurel put her pillow?

Between her boots?

In the bathtub?

On the fish tank?

In the tree?

On her bed!

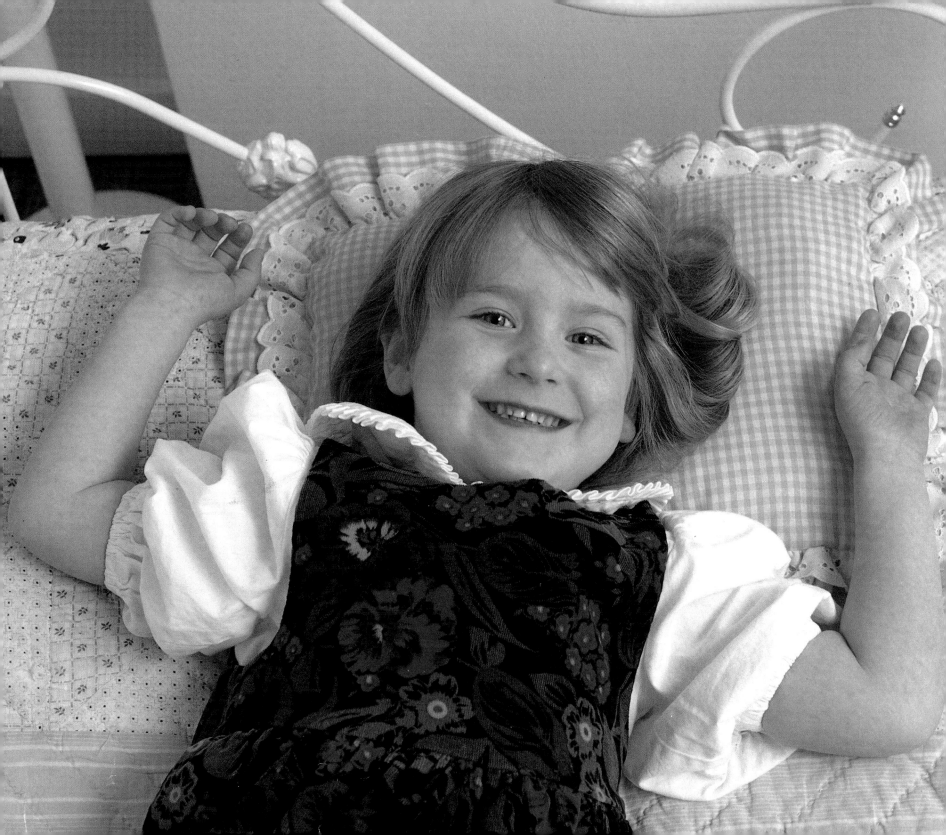

Where does Matthew put his jacket?

On the dog?

Behind the hamster's cage?

Under the lamp?

In the refrigerator?

In the closet!

MARGARET MILLER is a freelance photographer who lives in New York City with her husband, two children, and three dogs. She traces her love of photography to her childhood. "My mother is a wonderful photographer and I grew up in a house filled with family photographs. I especially loved being with her in the darkroom. I also spent many hours looking through two very powerful books, *The Family of Man* edited by Edward Steichen, and *You Have Seen Their Faces* by Erskine Caldwell and Margaret Bourke-White. After college I worked in children's book publishing for a number of years. I had always taken photographs of my family and I was fortunate in realizing my goal of combining my two long-time interests—photography and children's books."

Margaret Miller is the author/photographer of *Whose Hat?, Who Uses This?, Whose Shoe?*, and the *My First Words* board books; and the photographer for *Ramona: Behind the Scenes of a Television Show; Safe in the Spotlight; The President Builds a House; Your New Potty;* and *My Puppy is Born.*

6